THE NEW BIZARRO AUTHOR SERIES
PRESENTS

I0566376

HUMAN
FISH

BENJAMIN DEVOS

ERASERHEAD PRESS
PORTLAND, OREGON

ERASERHEAD PRESS
P.O. BOX 10065
PORTLAND, OR 97296

www.eraserheadpress.com
facebook/eraserheadpress

ISBN: 978-1-62105-289-0
Copyright © 2019 by Benjamin DeVos
Cover design copyright © 2019 Eraserhead Press

Printed in the USA.

1

The Human Fish took a smoke break after the dolphin show.

He floated across the aquarium tank, letting the nicotine do its work.

The dolphin swam up and the Human Fish puffed into its blowhole.

The audience watched on in horror.

They'd never seen a fish smoke before.

As a mammal, the dolphin didn't bother them when it choked up a black blob of sludgy saliva.

But the Human Fish was only part mammal.

He was a half-man, half-fish hybrid.

He took a drag and blew a lazy smoke ring one after the other toward a child leaning over the tank.

Some people clapped.

Others shook their heads, expressions reflecting frustration at the unanticipated smokiness; they turned and left in twos and threes.

He offered the child a puff of his cigar, but a curmudgeonly old man pushed him away.

A teacher escorted her group of schoolchildren out of the exhibit.

She called the Human Fish a lousy role model.

The Human Fish didn't even know what a role model was.

He was still figuring out the world of man and learning through trial and error.

He'd recently left the sea to search for his father.

Growing up with a single trout as a mother was difficult.

She was a good mom, if not overbearing.

Her constant suspicion of civilization drove the Human Fish crazy.

She had an acute fear of the unknown, of the surface where hooks and nets hung like death markers.

Ironically, her paranoia only drove the Human Fish further toward the world of man.

He'd seen a few humans with bleached hair and bronze skin that rode boards through the surf.

Once he saw a man catch a violent wave that coiled with the electricity of an eel and shocked him into the water.

The Human Fish went to see if the fall injured him, but the surfer retreated as if he'd seen a demon emerging from the abyss.

He made a habit of asking his mother about these men, but each time she would change the subject.

She would say something like, "Back in my day, there was never this much algae."

The other guppies teased him for not having a father.

They called him "Land Bastard."

The elder fish treated him as a lost soul cobbled together by scales and semen that didn't belong in their habitat.

Their exclusion frustrated the Human Fish, and by his early teens, it manifested in full-blown rebellion.

He started hanging out past curfew with the sharks, a group of fish hated by everyone and trusted by no one.

That only lasted until he cut his foot walking across sea glass.

The sharks swarmed at first sight of blood and tried to chew his leg off.

After that, he hung with the reptiles.

They would get stoned on the sun and watch the panorama of sky pinwheel in a haze through the water.

One day, he witnessed a turtle get caught in a net filled with floating packets of white sand.

He cut the turtle loose with his overgrown fingernails, and out of curiosity jabbed a hole in one of the bags.

The white sand dissolved in a cloud around the Human Fish's head.

Immediately, heat and frenetic energy coursed up his spine and through the tip of his skull.

His synapses misfired, and the world readjusted itself in a spectrum of dizzying color palettes.

He felt like he could do ten billion underwater backflips in a row without getting tired.

The turtle tried to lick the remaining residue from inside the bag.

The plastic wrapped around the turtle's head and trapped him again.

But the instant the white sand touched the turtle's tongue, it tore itself free with its sharp turtle beak.

It did a strange turtle dance that involved rotating its flippers in spontaneous rotations.

The Human Fish did the same, spinning his arms like boat propellers, floating up, up, up until he hit the surface and slowly drifted back down.

It was the best and worst sensation he'd ever felt, and his first instinct was to exploit it.

To finally have power in a world that shunned him for his otherness.

He went into business with the turtle, selling the white sand to crustaceans and other bottom feeders.

The hermit crabs liked to get high and play shell roulette.

It was like musical chairs, only with shells, and the crab who didn't find a shell in time had to streak naked across the seafloor.

Soon every creature knew, if you wanted to feel your face implode from a bliss-inducing rush of blood to the gills, the Human Fish was the half-man to talk to.

The problem was that the turtle didn't have much self-control and dug into the supply.

He wanted to go fast like the other reptiles and snorted white sand to get an edge.

He did line after line, losing weight and gaining speed, losing brain cells but keeping pace.

Then one day, the Human Fish swam over to the turtle's nest to get the money he owed.

He knocked on the turtle's shell, but nobody answered.

He knocked and knocked, but still nothing.

The Human Fish took matters into his own hands and reached inside of the shell for the money.

That's when he felt the turtle's cold, lifeless skull, bobbing like a buoy in the current.

The Human Fish freaked out.

He repeated the phrase, "It's okay, it's okay, it's okay," in his head and swam around in circles.

He was fearful, and a bit inebriated himself.

He dragged the turtle to a nearby reef and buried it under a mound of sand.

He dumped the rest of his supply in the deep sea and laid low back home.

In the coming days, other sea creatures asked the Human Fish about the turtle.

No one had seen him around the ocean basin for a while, and they were growing concerned.

The Human Fish acted like everything was okay, but his mother's intuition was never wrong.

She knew something was amiss.

Between his withdrawal from the white sand and the death of the turtle, he was coming apart at the seams.

He didn't know what to do.

He didn't want to break his mother's heart or pay the consequences for the turtle's death.

After all, selling the white sand was his idea.

So he dug up the money he'd saved and swam away from home.

He left a note that said he was embarking on a divine mission from Poseidon to find out who his father was.

He hitched a ride on the back of a speedboat that hauled him to a pier off the coast of California.

It wasn't until he reached the shore and tried to open his eyes that the Human Fish realized he couldn't see above water.

The oxygen's pressure was too intense.

Keeping his eyes open for more than a few seconds made his corneas retract into his eye holes like two compressed balloons.

He staggered forward blindly until he found a surf shop and asked the clerk if she had anything to protect his eyes from the painful air.

The clerk gave him a pair of goggles.

He placed the suction cups against his face, and for the first time, he saw the world of man.

He saw the clerk staring at him with a stunned expression on her face.

Like he had gills growing out of his neck and scales up and down his arms, which he did.

Not to mention, he was nude.

The rest of him was average for a human.

He had two eyes, a nose, and hair that frizzed like a self-adhesive wig.

He walked out in a pair of flippers to hide his scaly feet, and a bathing suit to cover his nethers.

It was too hot to wear anything else.

He got rejected by many restaurants that went by the no shoes, no shirt, no service policy.

He survived by eating out of dumpsters and sleeping in the ball pit at the McDonald's PlayPlace.

It took a while, but the Human Fish realized that people in the world of man had to work to support a home.

They had jobs, and bills, and paid taxes.

Capitalism was a foreign concept, but the Human Fish knew he had to learn to live like a human.

It was a classic 'sink or swim' scenario.

He asked random people on the street whether they could give him a job.

"Can you give me a job? Can you give me a job? Can you give me a job?"

One stranger stopped to talk with the Human Fish.

She was an elderly woman with poor eyesight and saw nothing unusual about him.

She merely thought he was mentally handicapped.

She told the Human Fish about this thing that the hip young kids used to find jobs.

Something called the Internet.

There were places called libraries where people went to use the internet for free.

So the Human Fish walked to the library.

He asked the librarian to show him to the internet.

The librarian took the Human Fish to the computer lab.

She helped him log on and then left him to fend for himself.

He poked the monitor, but nothing happened.

There was a device in front of him with mechanical levers and mysterious symbols.

He understood nothing about what he was seeing.

It felt like a dream.

The Human Fish concluded that the internet was inside the monitor.

He tried to open it, pulling with all his strength, but the monitor wouldn't budge.

So he tried a different approach.

He lifted the monitor over his head, did a sort of half-jump, and slammed the computer on the ground.

It took a few tries until the monitor split open.

But all that was inside were a bunch of wires and metal plates, no internet, no jobs.

After the first couple slams, the people in the library broke into a panic.

They sprinted through the stacks screaming about a lunatic in the computer lab who was on a smashing spree and might be a terrorist.

The librarian called 9-1-1.

When the police showed up, they found the Human Fish hunched over, hand on his chin, analyzing the keyboard.

He wanted to know what these strange and mysterious symbols meant.

He held up the device to ask the officer for an explanation.

They mistook his movement for a threat, and the police tackled the Human Fish to the ground.

He flopped around, trying to resist, and one of the officers pulled out a Taser.

Electricity flashed from the prongs, and the Human Fish whimpered and curled up in the fetal position.

There was nothing that scared a creature from the sea more than electricity.

The police handcuffed the Human Fish and shoved him in the back of the paddy wagon.

They drove him to their station downtown.

He couldn't afford bail, so they put him in a cell Tipsy, the drunken, suicidal clown.

He spent the night listening to Tipsy crying in the corner of the cell.

His cries fluctuated between an inconsolable moan and spine-chilling laughter.

Fortunately, the police released the Human Fish from jail the next morning.

An anonymous fan posted his bail.

The story was all over the news: Half-Man Half-Fish Creature Smashes Computer At Local Library.

He walked out onto a street flocked by protestors.

They had picket signs that said "California PD is Fishing for Sport," and "Free the Human Fish."

The sudden wave of support overwhelmed him, but he knew this was an opportunity.

He walked through the crowd, smiling his sharp sets of teeth.

He asked each protester that he passed if they could give him a job.

"Can you give me a job? Can you give me a job? Can you give me a job?"

Some gave him money, others food, but nobody had any jobs to offer.

That was, until he made his way to the outer limits of the crowd, and met a chairperson on the aquarium's board of trustees.

He told the Human Fish that he was a longtime member of California Trout, a conservation and advocacy organization.

He said his mission was to ensure resilient wild fish thrived in healthy waters.

In the Human Fish, he saw the prospect to further his reputation among state activists.

And that's how the Human Fish started working the Dolphin Show.

He didn't even have to go through training.

He was fluent in dolphin and communicated with them better than the trainers.

It was a full-time job with salary and benefits, and just like that, the Human Fish became a functioning member of society.

The world of man knocked him down then embraced him, and the Human Fish played the part well.

He got an apartment, learned to drive a car, and filed for health insurance with both a doctor and a veterinarian.

He bought a gym membership that he never used.

He joined a book club but never actually read the book.

He found religion, but the whole 'man-god' thing made him uneasy.

He grew up believing God was the sparkling light in the sky.

He found out soon upon entering the world of man that the light was not God, but something else.

Something he still couldn't comprehend.

Other things about the world of man made him uneasy.

He shuddered every time he saw a smokestack spewing pollution that blackened the air.

The needless violence that wasn't part of the food chain troubled him.

His biggest pet peeve was the way humans owned other animals, specifically dogs.

The way they walked them around on leashes

and picked up their feces in transparent plastic bags angered him.

The longer the Human Fish stayed in the world of man, the more disenfranchising it became.

He started boozing, showing up to work late and hungover, and taking unauthorized smoke breaks mid-show.

He got an anchor tattoo on his bicep, and shortly after got a harpoon on the other arm.

He got hooks pierced through his cheeks and had his teeth blackened.

He blasted nihilistic goth music at all hours of the night until the neighbors called the cops.

He hardly ever left home unless it was to go to work or the bar, and occasionally a strip club.

He didn't know what else humans did when they got sad, or how they got over being sad.

He was lonely and longed for the community he had back in the ocean.

The only way that the Human Fish could sleep was in a bathtub filled with water, like a vampire in a coffin.

Some nights he swore the turtle's ghost was haunting him.

He heard it racing around the bathroom high on white sand.

He was waiting for the Human Fish to fall asleep so he could seek swift revenge by biting through his jugular with his sharp turtle beak.

The Human Fish wanted to go back in time to that moment when he found the turtle tangled up in netting.

They would swim away without ever touching the stuff.

But it was too late for that.

The Human Fish had to live with the consequences of his actions whether he liked it or not.

He'd crossed the imaginary boundaries between worlds, and there was no going back.

He felt rudderless, lost in the center of a vast, vulnerable space where the horizon shone in every direction.

The world was open to an endless amount of possibilities that were every bit as complex and unfathomable as the ocean itself.

It was a roadmap to ruin.

A nightmare realm where he had no control over his destiny.

If he made the wrong choice, took the wrong turn down the wrong alley, or ended up in the wrong place at the wrong time, he chanced falling into a bottomless pit.

But that was a risk he had to take.

2

After the final dolphin show of the day, the Human Fish toweled off and proceeded to the aquarium's food court for dinner.

During his time living in the ball pit at McDonald's, he'd grown addicted to the grease and oils and sugar of fast food.

Now he ate fatty animal flesh for every meal.

His skin was breaking out into irritated purple pus bubbles that burst at random times.

He was chowing down on a double cheeseburger when a fat little boy with a pin-sized head and bloated cheeks waddled over.

He demanded that the Human Fish give him an autograph.

This happened sometimes, and it perplexed the Human Fish.

He didn't understand the human custom of commemorating a moment by marking a sheet of paper.

The Human Fish gripped the boy's pen in his fist and stabbed holes in his aquarium program until it was shredded.

The little boy's mother pulled out her camera and told them to "say cheese."

The boy smiled in the nervous, questioning way that children do.

His face stretched back to his ears in a cheery grin.

His eyebrows pointed down like harpoons drawn and ready to fire.

The human didn't smile or say cheese.

He looked miserable in most pictures or otherwise distracted.

When the mother showed them the picture, the little boy said, "scary."

The Human Fish laughed.

He hadn't realized that ketchup from the burger was all over his face.

He looked like a shark that had just finished feasting.

Suddenly, he seized the little boy's shirt sleeve and wiped his face off with it.

The little boy trembled like a bomb about to ignite and burst into tears.

The mother scooped the boy up in her arms and scolded, "Bad Fish! Bad Fish!"

The Human Fish fled the scene and finished his burger on the drive to the strip club.

It was his third night in a row at The Bearded Clam.

He'd gone there out of curiosity after spying their advertisement from the highway.

It was a sign with a hairy mollusk with eyeballs

unfolding to expose a pearl before snapping shut and winking.

The strip club was a place where neckless, beer-swilling men with sausage fingers went to fondle themselves.

At first, the bouncer tried to turn the Human Fish away on account that he was shirtless.

His scales made him appear like he was carrying a contagion, possibly leprosy.

But a group of dancers vouched for him.

They all thought the Human Fish was the cutest thing they'd ever seen.

They were some of the most striking people he had come across.

There was Pimples, a pouty, emaciated ex-cheerleader whose diet was comprised of weight-loss pills and corn chips.

Part of her shtick was rubbing the corn chips into her face until they crumbled into her open blemishes.

She explained, "The only way to make it as a stripper is to exaggerate yourself, so you stick out from the rest."

A putty-faced woman with big fake knockers and a cheetah-print bikini looked like she may be nearly a hundred years old.

She pinched the Human Fish's cheek like a fond grandmother.

They were all beautiful in their own way.

But there was one girl in particular.

A super-vixen.

The Human Fish wasn't sure how old she was in human years, but she seemed young.

She had a face that burned like dusk.

Her autumn-hued eyebrows and ultraviolet lipstick glowed like radium in the darkness.

She had stringy hair dyed green that flowed down her back and reminded the Human Fish of seaweed.

She had more tattoos showing than freckled skin, and lip rings that reminded him of fish hooks.

Her name was Destiny.

He approached her how the little boy had approached him, shy and filled with wonder.

She was sitting on the lap of a saggy old man with a lit cigarette lolling from his lips.

When the Human Fish caught her eye, she leaped up from the saggy old man's lap and gave him a playful poke in the ribs.

"Well, look who's back. It's the fish man."

The Human Fish tried to think of something witty to say, but all he could manage was to shake his head and blush.

A heavenly warmth rippled through his belly like the sun through the waves.

Destiny led the Human fish to an area draped in red velvet curtains and bathed in a fog of murky yellow light.

She eased him down onto a leather couch that stuck to his moist serpentine flesh.

She mounted him and rubbed up against his scales without flinching at their slimy touch.

She shoved her fingers into his tangled hair and pulled him into her breasts.

Her grinding was equal parts rough and tender.

"You know what we call these?" she asked pointing

at her knit stockings, "Fishnets."

The Human Fish was anxious and excitable.

Oily perspiration oozed from every pore.

He inhaled her natural, unperfumed musk.

She smelled like peaches that had been sitting out in the heat for too long.

The sculpt of her bust heaved like octopus heads on the verge of popping.

He reached out toward her breasts as if he'd seen a worm at the end of a hook, but this wasn't Destiny's first rodeo.

She smacked the Human Fish's hands away and slid down beside him on the couch, laughing.

"You can look, but don't touch," she whispered in his ear.

"Not that I'd it from you. But I don't want these other perverts thinking I'm a free squeeze bag."

Destiny went to the bar and returned with a tequila sunrise for herself and a sea breeze for the Human Fish.

The Human Fish puckered his rubbery lips at the tartness of the drink.

A stripper with a flat kitty-face passed.

Her stomach was swollen like a boob or a pus bubble.

She wore a bedazzled respirator mask that hid the lower half of her face.

She strutted around like a rooster in a teeny miniskirt, short, velvet, and revealing.

The Human Fish asked Destiny why the stripper wore a mask.

Destiny said, "She's having a baby, and this is a toxic environment."

The Human Fish cringed, and Destiny laughed.

She said, "Tell me about yourself. I want to know everything."

As they traded stories and flirted, he realized how much they had in common.

They were both raised by single parents, for the Human Fish his mother, and for Destiny her father.

They grew up looking for trouble, and both eventually found it.

Destiny told the Human Fish about her time as an addict.

Her drug of choice was heroin.

That was, until the night she overdosed and almost lost her life.

She shot up some fentanyl-laced junk with her ex-boyfriend in a porta potty at a Juggalo carnival.

When she woke up, a man with his face painted like the devil was giving her mouth to mouth.

The Human Fish told her about the turtle, how he got high on their supply and ended up in a shallow grave.

He told her there wasn't a day that went by that he didn't think about his poor dead friend.

He told her about the turtle's ghost, how the other night he finally saw it.

He told her that existence didn't end after death, but it did change.

The turtle, for example, shed its shell in the afterlife.

It flew around like a deflated balloon or demonic pancake, hissing curses that the Human Fish would suffer the same fate.

Destiny said that every day the living dead came to watch her dance.

She said the ghosts were her sleaziest customers, and that once people died their sexual appetites only seemed to increase.

They carried with them all of the incurable STD's from their past lives.

It disturbed the Human Fish.

He assumed that death would cure sexual desire and venereal disease.

"If only," said Destiny. "My life would be way simpler."

The Human Fish looked around at the paper-skinned men, drooling and breathing hard.

They seemed to glide across the floor without touching the ground.

The buxom beauties attracted them like a tractor beam.

The unnerving specter of their automatic, ethereal movements gave him the creeps.

"Wait," said the Human Fish, "These are actual ghosts?"

"Of course," said Destiny, "I thought you knew. Before this place was a strip club, it was a bar called Davy Jones' Locker. The bar burnt down, and many people died, but the owner, Cristiano, somehow made it out alive. He opened this place, but the spirits of the dead never left. Luckily, I mostly work during the day. The ghosts only come out in the evening."

Destiny told the Human Fish that she was getting off at midnight and asked if he wanted to come over when she got off.

"What's your phone number?" she asked.

The Human Fish told her that getting a phone was one thing he still needed to do.

Destiny laughed.

"Then how will I reach you?"

The Human Fish told her that he would wait until her shift was over, and they could leave together.

He sat there and watched her dance for hours.

He thought about how he could watch her dance until his dying day.

And he would return in the afterlife as a ghost to watch her dance for eternity.

Destiny finished at the stroke of midnight and went to the changing room to get dressed.

She reappeared like a bat out of hell.

It was the first time that the Human Fish had seen her in clothes.

She was wearing a leather jacket, black bandana, and cowboy boots embellished with rhinestones that were peeling off.

It was a more hardened exterior than the Human Fish had seen from her, but he liked it.

Outside of the bar, there was a group of Hell's Angels parking their motorcycles in a row against the curb.

The bikers were all decked out in leather vests, black bandanas, and jeans.

Some of them had pistols and sawed-off shotguns strapped to their waists.

Others carried switchblades between their teeth.

Destiny told the Human Fish that the trigger-happy gunslingers ran drugs for Cristiano.

She said that back when she was an addict, she used to date the president of the motorcycle club.

They'd broken up very recently in fact.

She pointed him out.

He wasn't the biggest or the most rugged-looking outlaw in the bunch, but something was menacing in his eyes.

The Human Fish could tell that the guy was out of his fucking mind.

He kept looking back over his shoulder to make sure the biker-ex with the crazy eyes wasn't following them.

Destiny walked led him to the back lot where she parked.

There behind the rear of the dumpster, was a slab of menacing machinery that looked like an iron horse.

It was a chopper, a big, heavy, ugly motorcycle saddled and ready to gallop through the night.

Destiny climbed aboard the beast and patted the seat behind her.

"Hop on."

He tried, straining one flipper, then the other over the ridges.

He adjusted his ass until it fit into the curve of the seat.

Destiny wrapped the Human Fish's arms around her waist.

He could feel his tremors passing through her torso.

"A little nervous, eh?" she laughed and reached into the satchel on the side of the motorcycle.

"It's better we use this in case you accidentally let go."

She pulled out a dog leash and hooked one end around the Human Fish's throat.

She cinched the other end beneath her breasts.

The Human Fish wondered whether this was more dangerous.

He imagined falling and the leash stiffening and

snapping his neck.

Destiny would follow in a death spiral against the concrete.

The Human Fish didn't question her though.

He had never ridden a motorcycle.

Maybe there was something he didn't know that would explain the logic of the leash.

Those thoughts disappeared in a split second once they got on the open road.

Destiny zigzagged back and forth between six lanes of traffic at high speed.

The Human Fish squeezed tighter.

His entire body stiffened as if in rigor mortis, but he felt more alive than ever.

The human part of his brain pumped out intoxicating amounts of adrenaline.

The fear turned to excitement, then ecstasy.

He slowly inched one arm back, then the other, and once they were in a clear lane, lifted his arms up.

For that moment he was not a human nor a fish, but a bird in flight.

He soared down Hollywood's boulevard of broken dreams, through discolored oxygen and exhaust, past prostitutes puffing on pipes, drag queens with mohawks and cadaverous meth addicts with carved X's in their foreheads, breakdancing for spare change.

They were the creatures that lived in the darkness.

Once the sun set, they rose as one to ravage the night.

It all looked so blurred and twisted and cold.

He looked up at the enormous sky and the bright full moon and pink clouds that filled it.

He felt like the physical equivalent of a scream in the night.

They passed abandoned buildings with the windows smashed out, porn shops and liquor stores, cemeteries and insane asylums, the seedy tattoo parlor where Destiny got inked.

They drove straight into the heart of depravity until they reached an old ranch house at the end of the road.

Destiny parked in the backyard.

There was uncut grass grown thick and high that tickled their ankles.

The dizzying comedown made the Human Fish wish that Destiny kept vomit bags in her satchel.

There were doors to a storm cellar buried underneath a pile of corroding iron waste pipes.

Destiny yanked them out of the way and opened the doors.

She held a finger to her lips and said, "Be quiet, my dad's bedroom is right upstairs."

The Human Fish followed her through the doors and shut them behind him.

Destiny turned to him in the darkness, murmured in a low, ominous tone, "Abandon all hope, ye who enter here."

3

The Human Fish tripped over his flippers and into the dark.

He fought to fit through the narrow corridor that led into the basement.

Destiny turned on a black light lamp mounted on the wall and told the human to relax.

She left to change into something more comfortable.

While she was gone, he explored the shadow-swathed room.

It was a cement abyss, windowless and devoid of furniture aside from a mattress on the floor.

It looked more like a cave than a living space.

There was rot in the cobwebbed-corners that showed through to the dirt and worms that lay beneath.

It was a writhing and gleaming portrait of indestructible life.

The Human Fish sat on the mattress and thought about how much of Earth was a barren, dead planet.

One big desert.

He wondered whether there were other Human Fish in ancient times.

He imagined a species of super-advanced, hyper-intelligent, green-skinned, shaman-like beings that lived in verdant forests and tamed scorpion creatures that they rode around at festivals that occurred every few Earth days.

It was almost too pure to visualize.

Destiny returned wearing a silk robe.

Her hair was pulled back in a good-girl ponytail, makeup removed.

She looked different without her eyes mired in a bog of runny black eyeliner.

Without the nicotine stains around her lips.

Like an angel.

She had two mugs filled with ice and corn liquor, legit moonshine that her father distilled in a bathtub.

The Human Fish was still woozy from the motorcycle ride but accepted the drink.

Destiny sat down next to him and pressed play on a clock-radio sitting at the foot of the mattress.

Out of the speakers came a crackling that sounded like a pin scratching against a vinyl record.

"You know what that sound is?" asked Destiny.

The Human Fish shook his head.

"It's fire. Sometimes I listen to it when I'm trying to sleep. It relaxes me."

She asked him what he was thinking about while she was gone.

He made something up about the weather, and

how Los Angeles dried out his skin and his nose was always crusty.

Destiny told him about a crazy news story she'd seen on television about a flood in Georgia.

She said one guy was floating on a hollow wooden barrel in the middle of the deluge.

He was holding up a doomsday placard and proclaiming the end of the world.

The Human Fish found it hard to understand how a flood would constitute an apocalyptic premonition.

Then again, a fish in the ocean did not fear the rain.

He took a sip of the moonshine and grimaced, wondering if humans ever adapted to the poison.

As they drank, their bellies warmed, and their tongues loosened.

Destiny opened up about her past.

She decided early on that ordinary life was not for her.

She quit school, but not before spreading gonorrhea to half of the junior class, a feat she took great pride in.

She threw caution to the wind, stripped naked and blasted off into the wonderful world of adult entertainment.

"I never had any role models to look up to. I made my own path."

There's that term again, thought the Human Fish, "role model."

The Human Fish talked about his mother.

He said that she was a great parent that did everything to provide a healthy, stable life for him.

He talked about how they used to be buddies and do stuff together.

She used to take him to the kelp forest as a child.

He was always afraid of getting lost, and would only walk through if he could hold her flipper.

She'd sing to him while they walked, and by the time the song was over, they'd be in the clearing on the other side, safe and sound.

He told Destiny how he felt shame for leaving his mother behind.

He'd grown up, gotten a job, a stable lifestyle, everything that she ever wanted for him.

Yet, for all she knew, the Human Fish was filleted in a sushi restaurant somewhere.

He had yet to redeem himself for the damage he'd done, and the agonizing burden of interminable guilt weighed on him.

Destiny told him about her father.

He worked as a cross-country trucker.

She told the Human Fish that her father often ingested hallucinogenic mushrooms.

Drugs helped distractions in the periphery fade so he could focus solely on the road and driving.

They kept him from going insane.

Destiny said that her father saw himself as a free-spirit pulled toward a point in the future.

That's how she got her name.

"What about your mom?" asked the Human Fish.

Destiny sighed and took a sip of her moonshine.

"Long story short, she smoked some angel dust, stabbed my dad, set the house on fire, and got committed to a hospital for the criminally insane. She died a few years ago. Brain cancer. Basically, my dad raised me by himself."

The Human Fish put his clammy hand on her shoulder.

He said, "If there's anything that I've learned, it's that every creature is vulnerable to the savagery of nature. It's an energy that surges not only in the wild but also in the very core of our being as human animals."

Destiny appeared detached, eyes drifting in a moment of intense reflection.

"I remember watching her attack my dad. It was as if she had left her body and was inhabited by another, more violent and evil person. I guess that's the way of the world. People are born as tiny wrinkled fetuses and leave possessed by demons."

She paused to take another sip of her drink, and the Human Fish did the same.

He slurped the last bit of alcohol, then sucked an ice cube into his mouth.

He immediately spat it back out, wincing at the coldness.

Destiny laughed and poured him a refill.

When she leaned over, she rested her head on his shoulder.

She cooed in his ear as the moonshine drizzled and his heart ballooned.

"He's a tough bastard, my dad. There was this one time when I was a kid. We went to see some movie, I can't even remember, and this guy a few rows away from us started masturbating. Oh, it was the Lion King, I remember now. Before I knew it, my dad leaped back there and was punching the guy in the head. Almost beat him to death. I can still picture the smile on his face as the man lay there bloodied and bashed. He was so proud of himself. I was proud of him too for defending the kids in the audience. On the drive home though, he told me the reason he attacked was that the guy was jacking it to animals. He took that incredibly personal for some reason."

The Human Fish was squirming by the end of the story, and Destiny tugged him closer.

She whispered softer, so close that he could feel her hot breath entering his gills.

"I did a lot of bad things when I was with the Hell's Angels. I slashed tires, mugged rich people, stole cars, killed a cop. I was hyperactive and didn't have much supervision, you know? Like I've owned a gun since I was thirteen. I started smoking in elementary school. I've always lived in the moment. I didn't plan any of it."

The Human Fish said, "No parent ever raised their child to be a screw-up. It's the not-raising that's the problem."

Destiny smiled.

"Are you called me a screw-up?"

The Human Fish smiled back.

"I'm saying it's not your fault."

She reached across his lap and put her hand on his thigh.

The Human Fish gulped in a fashion that was more fish than man.

His Adam's apple struggled to readjust in his throat.

He copied her, reaching his clammy hand under her arm to touch her thigh.

He had no idea what to do next.

He was following her lead.

She slid her palm toward his crotch, and he did the same.

He traced his fingers along her tribal tattoos, setting them ablaze.

Her skin was soft and tender.

Lambs would lie down in beds of her skin.

She teased her fingers like octopus tentacles above his waistline.

Then suddenly, she grabbed him by the gills.

She kissed him hard with tongue and teeth.

She pushed him flat on the mattress and flopped on top, holding him down by the wrists as they locked lips.

The Human Fish kept his eyes open while they kissed, and felt self-conscious that Destiny's eyes were closed.

He was about to interrupt their lovefest to ask if she thought he was ugly when he heard something.

The Human Fish was acutely attuned to sound waves.

He heard a creak from the floorboards overhead that doubled as the basement ceiling.

There was a warning signal in his head.

It reverberated like the roar of the ocean one hears when listening to a seashell.

He pulled away and raised his otoliths like a dog pricking its ears.

Destiny violently grabbed him by the hair and pulled him back in for more deep kissing.

The Human Fish imagined his mouth fusing with hers, their organs functioning as one.

He closed his eyes and listened to the crackle of the fire.

He saw the flames behind his goggles.

The passion between them grew hotter until it became a blaze of sadness and lust.

There was a groan as the basement door opened, but the Human Fish was too distracted to hear it.

His eyes were closed.

He couldn't see the silhouette rising from the darkness.

He barely noticed the footsteps, or the hand reaching for the scruff of his neck.

And for the first time, the Human Fish felt what it was like to be reeled in.

4

The Human Fish thrashed like a drowning child caught in the undertow.

He struggled to break free, but he couldn't fight the excruciating yank of his hair.

He was dragged up the stairs like a ragdoll, knocking his head against each individual step.

A door opened, and he found himself blinded by the light of a bright white kitchen.

The fluorescence felt like a pair of angry jellyfish suction cupped to his eyes and stinging them mercilessly.

Destiny burst through the door screaming, "Daddy stop! Get off of him, you shithead!"

The Human Fish's vision adjusted.

The first thing that he saw was an old gray dog with three legs, huddled on a mat in the corner of the kitchen.

It tried to bark at the Human Fish, but it was too weak.

He went to wrench the muscular tentacle from around his throat, but it was anaconda tight.

He'd never thrown a punch and didn't know how else to grapple free from his assailant.

He floundered like a fish out of water, flopping from side to side.

The chokehold grew tighter.

Tension rose from his solar plexus up through his throat.

His face turned blue.

His adrenal gland went into overdrive.

He oozed gooey oil out of his oversized pores.

His skin grew slippery, and the grip around his neck slackened long enough for Destiny to save him.

She tore the attacker's arm away with her teeth, snarling and ripping his flesh as she pulled him away.

The Human Fish gasped for breath and dashed to the sink, dunking his head in the dirty dishwater.

The attacker palmed Destiny's face like a basketball and pushed her off.

He yanked a knife from the drawer and gave a battle cry that was shrill and tinny and full of rage.

The Human Fish responded in kind, bleating like an angry goat and hurtling toward him.

They were rushing toward one another with the force of a thousand waves, but the Human Fish hit harder.

He knocked the knife away with a wild arm chop and was again caught up grappling with the man.

The man yelled, "Who the fuck are you," and clawed at the Human Fish's face.

He pulled off the Human Fish's goggles like a villain peeling off the mask of a superhero to reveal their identity.

The Human Fish battled the pressure building against corneas and looked his attacker in the eyes.

Both of them stopped and stared.

It was like looking in a mirror.

He took in every detail of the man's face, could hear the gasp of his lungs and the quick pace of his heart.

He knew by instinct that the molecules exchanged between their breaths were the same.

It was one of those rare visionary moments, like love at first sight, where people have an instant revelation of seeing themselves in another.

They realized, hands still coiled around each other's necks, that they were father and son.

Sparks flew between their eyes.

A bond forged in those fleeting seconds like their flesh had infused and refused to let go.

And at that same moment, Destiny whacked the man across the back with a cast-iron skillet.

He fell head-first through the drywall, his jaw piercing like a torpedo that sent dust flying.

He pushed himself out, hair askew, showing how he'd attempted to camouflage his bald head.

His puka necklace snapped and sprinkled cone snail shells across the floor.

He was out of breath and snorted up excess phlegm through his nostrils.

He reached into his pocket and pulled out an inhaler, and took a deep huff of the gas to relax his lungs.

His lips were bloodless, thin, and gasping for air like, well, a fish that had been dragged to shore.

His mushroomed stomach heaved.

The pajama pants around his chubby thighs

looked like stretched sausage casings wedged in the crack of his butt.

Liver spots blotted his leathery skin.

Wrinkles cornered his beady eyes

"Don't look at me," he said, panting, "Give me a second."

His tone was brittle.

The Human Fish was bleeding from his nose.

Destiny was crying, and the old gray dog was whining.

Bleeding and crying and whining.

Destiny's father looked like he might keel over and die.

He cracked his knuckles like a butcher snapping chicken wings.

He turned to Destiny and said, "Sugarlump, be a good girl and grab papa an ice pack?"

"Fuck you!" Destiny yelled.

He leaned toward the Human Fish.

"I guess introductions are in order. The name's Jim Hurley."

He held out his hand to shake, but when the Human Fish reached his clammy palm forth, Jim held out his fist to bump instead.

"Germs," he said, sitting on the floor, still panting.

"So either I'm hallucinating, or you're Taffy's boy?"

The Human Fish was confused.

Jim saw the expression on his face and elaborated.

"We called her Taffy because her body was sweet and from salt water."

Too much information, thought the Human Fish.

"Taffy put out for all of us fisherman back in the day. She told us that if we stopped sticking our hooks down in your business, she would let us have sex with her. Ah, but that many years and brain cells ago. Never imagined she'd have a kid though."

Way too much information, thought the Human Fish.

"I guess she had a net in her belly, one that caught my sperm and morphed it into, well, you."

Way, way too much information, thought the Human Fish.

He hoped that finding his father would solve the riddle of his existence, but it only gave him more questions.

He was now hesitant to ask, not wanting to hear anything else sexual.

He wondered whether Jim saw him as his offspring or as some human flotsam that washed up on his stoop.

Jim said, "Well, make yourself at home. You should know that the toilet's clogged. I'm going to take a whiz out back."

He took the old gray dog with him, leaving his offspring alone in the kitchen together.

The Human Fish could hear the stream of piss from Jim and the dog over the deafening silence in the kitchen.

Destiny spoke up first.

"Thank God all we did was kiss," she said.

The Human Fish didn't respond, and after a minute she went to get a broom to sweep up the crumbled drywall.

The Human Fish took the opportunity to get a better look at the upstairs.

There was a bathtub separating the kitchen from the living room that reeked of alcohol.

There was a bedroom to the left with the door cracked open.

The Human Fish peeked inside and saw a mattress on a platform up near the ceiling.

Underneath was shoved full of garbage, from empty milk cartons to lottery tickets.

There was a closet with a toilet, and the smell emanated like shit-scented perfume.

The living room was even more unsettling.

Sport fishing heads lined the walls.

Stuffed, mounted salmon on wooden plaques.

A six-foot swordfish with its sword nose poking out so that any passerby might poke their eye out.

There were dust laden mouse traps with moldy peanut butter and tiny skeletons.

There were heavy plasticized curtains that kept out the street lights and kept in the grime.

There were roaches cracked wide open and guts splattered against the plastic.

The Human Fish was sobering up and tuned in to his surroundings.

He listened to the zip of Jim's pants, and the curses he whispered under his breath.

Jim opened the door to the house, stuck his head in cautiously and walked through the kitchen.

The old gray hobbled in behind him, almost having his tail caught in the door.

He took a seat in the bathtub.

The Human Fish decided to make small talk this time to avoid another awkward situation.

Small talk was a trick he learned from the humans to ease the pressure of social interaction.

"So Destiny tells me you're a truck driver," said the Human Fish.

"Yeah, that's the day gig. The night gig too. It's not my lot in life is what I'm saying. I have bigger aspirations."

The Human Fish fidgeted, unsure what to ask next, but Jim went on for him.

"Lately, I've been having a ton of great business ideas. I think you specifically, will appreciate this. It's called 'Your Last Cruise.' It's where we take elderly people out to sea and pump them full of drugs and prostitutes for one last hurrah. Then we launch them out to sea as chum for the sharks."

Destiny came like a ghost through the wall, just suddenly there.

"Jesus dad, he doesn't want to hear about your crackpot inventions or your stupid business pitches."

The human had never been caught between disputing relatives before.

It made him cringe worse than the polluted air did.

"So I guess he doesn't want to hear about the self-cleaning robot that I've been building in my spare time."

There was sarcasm buried in his tone.

"You mean the scrap metal you stole from the junkyard? Jesus, you're delusional."

The Human Fish tried to ignore the arguing, and he started to ponder what led him to this moment.

He struggled to remember why he left the ocean.

Why would he make such a stupid decision?

That's when he saw it, the turtle's ghost circling overhead like a fan at top speed.

It was snapping its turtle beak rabidly, foaming at the mouth like a frosty beer.

The Human Fish dove and ducked for cover but it was too late.

The turtle was diving straight for him.

Destiny, who was keenly aware of ghosts, threw herself over the Human Fish as a blockade

She deflected the turtle.

It careened into the night like a car on the skids.

She helped him onto the easy chair in the living room and draped a blanket over his quivering legs.

Just then the dog came into the living room.

"Sorry, I should introduce you. This is Cranberry."

Cranberry inspected the Human Fish, unsure what to make of him.

"Anyway," Jim said, "Trucking ain't that bad. If you wanna see the world, driving a truck across the country is good a way as any."

Maybe it was the adrenaline from the night's events.

Maybe it was the alcohol.

Maybe it was the supreme feeling of guilt that he wished to appease, but the Human Fish asked, "Can you take me with you?"

Destiny shook her head as if to say "No, God, No!"

It was clear that, in her drunken state, she had embellished on the complementary aspects of her father.

He was actually a piece of shit, and this was a bad idea, but at that moment the Human Fish didn't care.

Jim scratched his crotch.

He adjusted his waistband and took a deep breath, sucking in his gut.

It was a simple answer, but also a binding contract that could not be undone.

"Sure, why the hell not?"

The answer echoed in the Human Fish's head.

"Why the hell not?"

He'd found out about hell when he tried religion.

It was a lake of fire that consumed people but didn't kill them, just let them suffer eternally with no escape.

It was no place for a fish.

It was no place for a human either.

There was a fiery sensation burning in his lungs.

The hot, stifling air caused him to dry heave.

Hell, he thought, didn't seem much different from his current situation.

"I leave tomorrow, at the crack of dawn, so I'll wake you up when it's time to go."

And just like that, the Human Fish's path was laid out before him.

He was given a one-way direction, and no longer had to worry about careening toward the edge without a plan.

Destiny was on the verge of tears and leaped across the room to hug him goodbye.

He felt her touch in a very different way than he had in the basement.

She had a surface roughness that she inherited from her father, clear as day, but underneath she was warm and sweet, if not a little chaotic.

The Human Fish could feel it pulsing through her skin.

Jim interrupted with a cough, and said "What's your name? I've gotta call you something."

The Human Fish had never thought about claiming a human name, thus completing his identity in the world of man.

Jim took the initiative.

"Igor," he said. "I'll call you Igor."

5

The Human Fish woke to the aroma of hardboiled eggs and some unidentifiable meat.

Neither of those things had been cooked.

It was more the smell of decomposition, ammonia, mold, and sulfur that wafted through the house.

His stomach was upset from the alcohol.

He lay there in a hungover haze trying to recount the previous night's half-remembered events.

The face of Jim was etched into his brain like a bad tattoo.

He remembered bits and pieces of their encounter, but they were scattered.

He sat up and stretched his legs, his groin numb.

He scratched at his chest hair and grazed a series of painful welts that weren't there the day before.

He heard footsteps from the adjoining room and lay back down.

He pretended to be asleep.

A beefy hand shook him.

"Time to hit the road, Igor. The early bird catches the worm, or the fish, hardy har har."

Jim wanted to leave before rush hour.

The trailer was loaded and ready to roll.

He poured coffee into a couple of mugs with a generous amount of sugar and curdled cream.

The Human Fish picked at a scab on his chest.

Blood oozed down in big red clumps.

"Damn bed bugs," said Jim.

The Human Fish asked if there was time for a shower, but Jim said no.

The Human Fish told him that he needed to be watered or else he'd dehydrate.

His skin would congeal like the cream in their coffee, and he may die.

"You're like a little desert flower," said Jim. "I'll hose you down on the front lawn."

He absorbed the water with the first beams of sunlight and let it all wash over him.

His pores filled with Vitamin D and moisture.

He was rejuvenated and wished that he had time to give Destiny a sober, less awkward goodbye.

But he was soaking wet, and Jim was on a tight schedule.

There was a garage a quarter mile from the house where the truck was parked.

By the time they got there, the Human Fish was dry.

Seeing the truck was enough to shock the water right out of him.

He'd thought that Destiny's motorcycle was a hulking beast of machinery.

It was like a minnow in comparison to Jim's whale of a truck.

The Human Fish stood open-mouthed and in awe of its girth.

He climbed aboard excitedly.

The interior proved far less remarkable.

The cab was filthy, claustrophobic, and cramped with garbage.

Fast food wrappers were scattered all over the floor along with a pile of dirty magazines.

On the ceiling was a poster of a full-frontal nude woman splayed spread eagle.

It smelled like exhaust, leather, alcohol, dog shit, dust, and armpits.

There was dog hair everywhere.

Cranberry perked up from the crevice behind his seat.

It was hot, and the Human Fish tried to roll down the window, but it stuck around the halfway point.

There was no air-conditioning, just the gasp of a fan with a dying motor.

Jim jammed the key in the ignition, and the engine sputtered to life.

Hands on the wheel, the Human Fish noticed the words "BORN FREE" tattooed across Jim's knuckles.

Jim reached for a chain hanging above the dashboard.

He hollered, "All aboard the express, next stop, your mom's house," and pulled.

The horn was more powerful than thunder and struck the Human Fish's eardrums like lightning.

It sounded like the throaty caw of a seagull that spotted a lump of soggy bread in the sand, times a thousand.

Jim ate a few mushroom stems and offered the rest to the Human Fish.

"You know, the trip is a lot more fun when you're tripping."

The Human Fish took a handful of caps from the bag and popped them in his mouth.

They tasted like dirt, and he swallowed them whole to avoid the chewy sensation of mud in his mouth.

They drove onto the highway, and after a few exits the mushrooms kicked in.

The highway kept going and going and going.

The interstate walls became a blur.

The Human Fish gave into the mantra of the spinning wheels.

He was sensitive to every tremor in the road, every divot.

They were speeding at an unspeakable velocity.

They were slicing like a knife through the heart of the country.

His pulse raced faster.

Dopamine and serotonin excreted from this brain at an exceeding rate.

It felt like being baptized into a new dimension.

His senses were overloaded by newfangled sights and scents.

They all stimulated new memories instead of bringing back old ones.

It was all foreign and scary but also new and exciting.

Yet, he didn't feel free.

He'd felt more unrestricted in the ocean, where he could explore uninhibited and without fear.

He wondered if Jim would survive if forced to live

in the ocean.

He asked Jim and looked into his pupils, black moons radiating past the whites of his eyes.

His body was pulsing like the ebb and flow of the sea.

He was a sea of flesh and muscle and tissue rippling through the metallic box.

Jim said that the illusions of law, order, and authority were all created to keep humans trapped by moral obligations.

As a result, freedom itself was a deception.

He said that there were no rules in the ocean, and if he lived there, he would drink and fuck and kill whenever he wanted.

The Human Fish closed his eyes and imagined a world where the borders were non-existent.

Where nothing was separating the humans from the fish.

He envisioned a giant shark in the sky, eating the clouds, and eventually devouring the sun.

Then in the darkness, it ate all of the humans in a river of blood.

Cranberry interrupted his daydream with a sloppy lick to the cheek.

The Human Fish thought how easy it must be to live a pet's life.

But he wasn't a pet, he was a human, a fish, a son, and his father wasn't his owner, but a stranger.

He knew it was better to clear the air early in the trip rather than let the tension build.

But in his hallucinogenic state, he could only muster one word, "Why?"

That's all he needed to say, "Why," and Jim knew.

He told the Human Fish the story of how he came to the docks and found his mother.

It all began when he heard about the Fish of Fortune.

Tales of it had been passed down for generations.

Its scales were made of amber, its eyes were gold, and inside, where the heart should be, was a precious jewel that was one of a kind and priceless.

There was a myth that it could be sold for billions, that you could buy a small country for its worth.

Jim wasn't sure if the Fish of Fortune existed, but he angled at the docks each day just in case.

This was when he was a younger man, before the truck driving days.

Back when he worked as a sleazy insurance salesman for the elderly.

He desired more for himself and believed the Fish of Fortune was his golden ticket to a better life.

He reeled in flounder, salmon, swordfish, but never anything of higher value.

Just as his faith began to wane, he met Taffy, a different kind of treasure.

She wasn't even latched to his hook but swam up to the dock of her own accord.

She offered Jim a deal.

If he stopped hunting in her habitat, she would let him have sex with her.

She guaranteed to be the best lay he ever had.

And by his account, she was.

He knew that their relationship could never transcend the carnal.

When she told him that she was pregnant, he fled

from the ocean like a tornado of sharks was chasing after him.

"I'm sorry, Igor," he said, looking away from the road just long enough to make eye contact.

His pupils were black holes sucking in the Human Fish.

"I didn't mean to abandon you, but hell, your mom seemed to do a good job raising you by herself."

The Human Fish thought about his mother, how she was undoubtedly sick with worry.

He considered the sacrifices that she made for him and was probably still making in his absence.

By now, she'd have sent out the entire sea to search for him.

She'd swim to shore and offer her orifices to fisherman in exchange for any information on where her son was.

"But don't you feel bad," asked the Human Fish. "How do you go through life without guilt for what you left behind?"

"The best answer I can give you is that I have shallow roots. That's how the truckers do it. These guys are diverse. On the radio, you'll hear everything from redneck hard-asses making racial jokes to men who have found Christ and are preaching the Gospel, to dick jokes, to pseudo-intellectuals talking politics. The one thing that they have in common is that they can't stay still for more than a little while. They travel where they want when they want. Otherwise, all of the shame and rage would bubble up, and society would suffer the consequences."

The Human Fish imagined the world of man as a

shit-spewing volcano.

It fouled up everything it touched.

He was overwhelmed and silent.

"Are you alright," asked Jim.

"Yeah," said the Human Fish. "I'm just not used to talking this much."

"It's what people do."

"I know."

Dusk came and went.

As the mushrooms wore off, Jim told the Human Fish that he needed to stop off for some beer and some sleep.

He pulled off on the shoulder of the road to a rundown motel hidden behind overgrown foliage.

"These motels are pretty raunchy, and the sanitation is questionable at best. There are some perks. If you wanna find some good company, and by that I mean sex, there are plenty of lot lizard around."

The Human Fish didn't want to talk about sex, but after discussing his mother, Jim was stuck on the topic.

"So Destiny, you didn't, you know," he pulled into a parking spot and stopped.

"Give the dog the bone, did you?"

The Human Fish looked down at the Cranberry, sleeping comfortably between their seats.

"Please tell me you didn't harpoon the salty longshoreman."

The Human Fish raised an eyebrow.

"Crab fish in the dead sea."

He raised the other eyebrow.

"Slam the salmon."

His mouth slanted open sideways.

"What I'm asking is if you released the Kraken."

The Human Fish didn't say anything.

He stared at the poster of the naked woman.

It was the first stagnant image he'd seen since hallucinating and sighed.

Jim said, "You a virgin, Igor?"

The Human Fish stayed silent.

His skin turned clammy, and his blood ran cold.

Jim slapped the dashboard.

"Holy shit," he howled, "You are!"

6

Out front of the motel, the Human Fish caught his first glimpse of a lot lizard.

It was crawling limb over nimble limb on the curb like some circus balancing act.

It leaped as soon as it saw the truck pull up.

At the same moment, Jim realized that the Human Fish was a virgin.

He thought it was some terrible twist of fate that there should be such an opportunity for sex so soon.

Jim knew that these opportunities were more few and far between than he made them seem.

He wasn't about to let the opportunity slip to have his son deflowered.

"Sometimes you've got to succumb to the wiles of the road," he said.

Then, to the Human Fish's horror, he popped the lock on the door and slid it open.

"Whatever happens on the road stays on the road."

The lot lizard was wearing a rebel flag crop top, washed out cutoff jeans, and a cowboy hat.

There was a hole in the back of her jeans where a spiky tale poked through.

Its skin was scaly like the Human Fish's.

She flicked her forked tongue and climbed aboard.

The heavy wave of musk from their bodies welcomed her into the hull.

Sniffing the Human Fish's odor, she hissed, "You smell like a virgin. Let me take your innocencsssssee."

The Human Fish seized hold of Cranberry and held him up in defense.

Cranberry had enough strength from sixteen hours of sleep to swipe a paw at the lot lizard.

The lot lizard flinched, giving the Human Fish enough time to open the passenger door and escape.

He ran to the motel lobby as fast as he could.

It smelled of burnt tar and moldy laundry.

The receptionist looked up from his magazine, saw the Human Fish, and scowled.

He had jet black hair, and thin lines shaved into his eyebrows.

He was wearing a black wife beater and oversized black capris tied with a rope around the waist.

He was barefoot, and his toes and legs were dirty.

He reached under the desk and pulled out a wooden baseball bat with the word Slayer carved into the side.

The Human Fish felt like a frightened interloper in a no-longer-friendly town.

Luckily, he wasn't left alone with the receptionist for too long.

Jim joined him momentarily, Cranberry in his

arms, out of breath.

Jim managed to yell, "Barricade the doors!"

The lot lizard came a few seconds later and tried to claw its way in.

It whipped its spiked tail against the doors that threatened to shatter with each strike.

"I've got this," said the receptionist, jumping over the desk, wooden baseball bat in hand.

As soon as the lot lizard saw him, she ran off screaming, and everybody in the lobby relaxed.

"You pussied out back there," said Jim, punching the Human Fish in the ribs.

"Those lot lizards are feistier than any other creature in the world, and that includes fish. Mermaids can be pretty wild, but you have to catch em at the right time."

The Human Fish rolled his eyes.

He knew that mermaids were a superstition.

"Let's go get some rest," he said.

The receptionist escorted them to a tiny room.

There was only one twin-sized mattress in the middle of the room, barely big enough to hold one of them.

The Human Fish looked in the bathroom, but there was no tub to sleep in.

Just a standing shower covered in mold.

The paint-chipped walls smelled like lead.

The ceiling planks were bent in from heavy rainfall and dripped black liquid.

The floors were broken tiles of what could have belonged to a community bathroom.

There were glyphs on the floor engraved by a knife or box cutter that and spelled out, "Spooge was here."

It wasn't long before the Human Fish realized humans check into motels to do unspeakable things that they would never do at home.

They spilled food and drink on everything.

Everything.

In three dimensions, not just horizontal surfaces.

Mac and cheese embedded in the drapes.

Chicken wing bones inside nightstand drawers, nestled comfortably next to Gideon's Bible.

And then, of course, there were bodily fluids to contend with.

Soiled diapers stuffed into a pillowcase.

A used condom stretched over the bathroom doorknob, deposit-side exposed so that the next hand to open the door would benefit from the donor's generosity.

People vomited on the bed, then covered it with a sheet as if nothing happened.

He quickly learned the difference between blood and barbeque sauce, snot and hair conditioner, a pool of urine and spilled beer.

There was a bowl of unwrapped, complimentary mints that Jim smuggled into his pockets.

He popped one in his mouth and offered another to the Human Fish, who declined.

"I don't know about you, but I'm starving. I should have packed more soup. I survive on soup."

"Soup?" asked the Human Fish.

"Yeah, mostly tomato. I can gulp it down in seconds. I don't need to heat it up, and it's instant fuel. Sometimes I resort to dog food, but that's rare."

The Human Fish wished he had some dog food to eat.

Or some soup.

Anything but bacterial-ridden mints.

"So are you familiar with the game, Rock, Paper, Scissors?" asked Jim.

The Human Fish was not familiar with this game.

"It's a game that people play when they're competing for something. As you probably noticed, there's only one bed, and there's two of us. So I'll show you how to play, and we'll work out who gets to sleep there."

Jim explained the basic rules.

Rock beat scissors, scissors beat paper, paper beat rock.

He showed him the hand motions and explained what best two out of three meant.

It was as close a match as they come.

The Human Fish started strong, with paper beating rock.

But he underestimated Jim the second time, again going paper.

Jim cut him into pieces with a sneaky scissors play.

It was all down to the last move.

The Human Fish went with his gut and slammed his fist down, but rock was met with rock.

A draw.

They went again.

Rock and rock.

Again.

Rock and rock.

This sick and twisted psychological game was becoming overwrought.

Both man and half-man half-fish were sweating profusely.

Neither refused to let their egos budge.

Rock and rock.

Again.

Rock and rock.

And then the Human Fish went for it.

He slid his palm into paper position, but Jim was a step ahead.

Scissors.

"You've gotta have balls to make it in this game," said Jim, crawling under the covers.

The Human Fish crashed on the floor, and as soon as his head hit the pillow, he could hear Jim snoring.

There may as well have been heavy artillery shooting off in the night.

The Human Fish couldn't sleep no matter how tightly he wrapped his head in blankets.

He was uncomfortable and scared.

He had no way to explain his fear upon seeing the cold expression of the turtle's ghost on the slanted ceiling.

He felt like a vampire wrapped in sheets, a person with secrets that had to be kept covered and hidden.

Their nights became routine in this way.

Jim always wore the same flannel pajama pants.

There was a tear in the crotch that his flaccid package hung through.

Jim would walk around the motel room farting and scolding himself.

And the Human Fish would sleep on the floor of each place they stayed.

Being together both asleep and awake made for eerie chemistry.

Their mentalities intermingled.

They shared spaces for extended periods, and left each other's company only to urinate, shit, or masturbate.

The Human Fish followed ritually, fraternally, in Jim's footsteps.

He tightened his jaw when his father did.

He rolled his eyes and sighed when he did.

It was childlike and innocent.

He was a sponge absorbing his father's mannerisms.

Even their speech tones and patterns began to sync up.

It came to the point where the Human Fish answered the radio to tell the base their coordinates.

They bonded that way.

It all seemed like a legitimate part of the process.

Of learning how to navigate the world from an unruly captain.

It all seemed to be going swimmingly until they reached Kansas.

Jim punched the steering wheel like a prizefighter going for the knockout.

The tedium of sitting in traffic opened up a black hole in his mind, and now fists were flying through the darkness.

Not to mention his bladder was on the verge of exploding.

After a day of driving, three cups of coffee, and no pit stops, he was ready to pee anywhere.

Not to mention they were lost.

Jim made a few wrong turns off the expressway trying to find a place to pee and ended up on a poorly-made dirt road.

It was filled with rocks and fallen tree branches that made him drive half the speed he would otherwise.

The Human Fish tried to sleep but couldn't while his head was pounding against the window.

Jim turned up the volume on the radio and punched the steering wheel to the beat.

He needed to pee before he lost his mind.

The Human Fish sat up and stretched.

Jim reached across his lap and took one of the empty coffee cups and undid the lid.

Handling the wheel with one hand, he used the other to unzip his pants and stick his flaccid member into the cup.

The release sounded like the roar of a blue whale cresting through a tidal wave.

Specks of pee came up and narrowly missed the Human Fish.

That was until the front tire hit an exceptionally large stone, and piss went everywhere.

Jim was soaked.

The Human Fish was hyperventilating.

They pulled over to the side of the road, and the Human Fish wondered why, even in such seclusion, a human wouldn't stop to piss in the open.

Jim got out of the truck and cursed.

He went off somewhere in the woods to change out of his wet clothes.

As he left, Cranberry started barking, and the Human Fish noticed a rat slide back through a crevice between the cab and the trailer.

He tried to reach through to grab it.

When that didn't work, he went back and

opened the trailer.

He'd never been inside and was curious to take a look.

There were crates piled high on all sides, and he climbed mountains to get to the front.

Near the cab, there was a wooden crate that had been chewed to pieces by vermin.

The Human Fish peeked inside to see if they were nested there.

Instead, he found something else.

He found drugs, meth, heroin, and weed wrapped in massive sheets of plastic like a dead body.

There was also a gun, not a small one either.

It had a rocket included.

There was another with a clip hanging down like an erect penis, filled with bullets.

The Human Fish panicked.

He knew Jim could return at any second to find him snooping.

He tried to go back to his seat, but something was holding him back.

He looked down and saw a cranked out pregnant mother rat biting down on his leg.

7

The Human Fish whimpered and shoved his fist in his mouth and so that he wouldn't scream.

He kicked at the mother rat.

She was probably thirty pounds, pregnant, and anchored to the floor.

Whether he attacked or retreated, his leg was in incredible pain.

The mother rat sunk her teeth deeper, ripping scales off, slicing through his meat.

He knew that if he fell to one knee, that she would spring for the jugular.

It was a waiting game.

As soon as the mother rat released her savage grip, he would whack her and climb out of reach.

She'd bitten down on the spot where his external armor ended, and his skin began.

Blood trickled down his leg into the aluminum siding of the trailer.

The Human Fish had experienced shark bites, but this was worse.

Sharks saw blood and went for the kill.

The mother rat seemed to revel in the mutilation.

She sucked down the plasma to nourish her unborn infestation.

The longer he waited to move, the more likely it was that Jim would discover him in the trailer.

For a split second, the mother rat cramped, and the Human Fish struck.

His jellied spine hoisted a gory flippered foot and punted the mother rat clear over the cargo.

He watched the furry rocket spinning end over end until it dropped directly into the chest of Jim, who fell like a soldier shot dead center by a sniper.

The mother rat squealed and scampered around in circles confused.

Cranberry wobbled to protect his owner.

The mother rat screeched to a halt.

It was dog versus rat faceoff, and the Human Fish was edging his way toward them as fast as he could.

Underweight and with only three legs, he would inevitably be torn to shreds by the mother rat.

The Human Fish scaled the cliff of boxes like an ancient mountain golem.

He clambered toward the opening at the end, hoping he wasn't too late to save Cranberry.

Luckily, Jim got his bearings in time to step in with a steel-toed Kodiak work boot.

The mother rat caught one glimpse of the metallic horror and made a break for a nearby sewer grate.

Jim chased after it, but even a wounded mother rat

had better lung capacity than him.

"Is Cranberry okay?" asked the Human Fish, slinking off of the trailer.

"Cranberry?" asked Jim. "What about me? That thing knocked me stiff. It could've killed me."

The Human Fish's leg was gushing blood to the point that he felt faint.

He said, "I knew it would take more than that hairball to take you out."

Jim squinted and looked over the Human Fish's shoulder at the open trailer.

He followed the trail of blood leading to the crate, the drugs, the rocket launcher.

The Human Fish stayed outside with Cranberry.

He pet him gently, afraid to break any bones.

Jim came out, torso naked, and offered his shirt to the Human Fish to wrap his wound.

"Okay you need to know, I'm not some down and dirty street criminal," said Jim, panting and taking a hit off his inhaler.

"This is real shit. What you saw in there is a matter of life and death. Not just for you and me, but for Destiny. There's more wrapped up in this than you know."

The Human Fish was quiet, but he was fluent in bullshit.

Taffy ain't raise no fool.

She taught him how to speak to humans in case of emergency.

She taught him how to intimidate, how to retaliate.

She taught him all of the turns of phrase he would need if ever in an altercation with a human.

But the Human Fish knew talk was cheap.

He punched Jim square in the chest.

He said, "Don't beat around the bush, motherfucker."

Motherfucker was used in the most literal sense possible.

"Tell me the whole truth, or I'm taking the bus back to LA."

Jim fell to one knee and took another hit off his inhaler.

"Alright," He said, "Here's the deal. Cristiano, the owner of the Bearded Clam where Destiny works, he's a bigtime drug dealer. One of the biggest in California and that means the country. He works with the Hell's Angels trafficking all kinds of narcotics. You name it, he moves it. I started running drugs for him shortly after Destiny started up at the club. I needed the cash. I've mostly done small jobs up until now, but this is the big one. This," he said motioning to the trailer, "Is my retirement fund."

The steely blue of his father's eyes rippled at that moment.

What were ordinarily beady and conniving were now desperate and swollen bags of water.

"Now don't think I won't cut you in. I'd usually offer ninety-ten since I'm taking most of the risk. But since you're my son, I'll cut you in for twenty percent of the profits. All we have to do is get the drugs to Chicago, and we're golden."

The Human Fish was in a quandary.

Maybe he'd craved someone to conspire with since the death of the turtle, but not like this.

Not drugs again.

Jim slammed the trailer shut and sauntered toward

where the mother rat escaped.

A thick trail of the Human Fish's blood led into the shrubbery.

"I wanna turn that rat to roadkill." said Jim, "A furry speedbump."

Hawks flew overhead and made scary noises with their chipped beaks.

It was the gruff, predatory sound of coldhearted existence.

The Human Fish imagined the tire of the truck wheeling over the mother rat's body.

He imagined it bursting open like a blood orange, oozing juicy nectar and the unborn fetuses spilling out and crawling over its scabbed bloody fur.

He walked back to the cab without a word.

He felt a revulsion that was tense and confusing.

A kind of discomfort like a clot in his brain that kept him off balance.

He was vulnerable; knowing that he needed Jim more than Jim needed him.

He despised him for it.

For having to rely on such a slug of drug-induced lethargic bitchiness to make his way through the world.

Jim drove onto the highway and got off as soon as he saw an exit, in search of a bar.

They both needed to loosen up, or else there was no chance of making it at all.

They found a watering hole called The Hog Wallow Pub and grabbed a table in the darkest corner.

The Human Fish ordered a Sea Breeze, and Jim got a piss-colored beer.

A little voice in the Human Fish's head grew louder with each drink.

It said, "Go back to the sea."

He opened his gullet and finished his drink.

The worst thing that could happen on this trip was death, he thought.

Everything else he'd experienced to some degree already.

Imprisonment, abandonment, disfigurement.

He accepted the possibilities long ago.

The primal contract was signed and sealed.

"Okay," said the Human Fish, face neutral and inexpressive, eyes locked on Jim. "I'm in."

The Human Fish followed the human custom and held out his hand to shake.

Jim smirked, leaned over the table.

He shook the Human Fish's hand with an enormous, beefy mitt that threatened to snap his wrist.

After a few more cocktails, they went out for cigarettes, and Jim told the Human Fish the plan.

"Since we're out west there are more inspection stations because of the border. They have drug dogs, x-ray equipment. They'll search us for narcotics, illegal aliens, bombs, whatever contraband they can find. Since you don't have any birth documents, they'll have a field day with you. We'll have to hide you in a fake compartment, maybe hollow out the walls or create a false cargo box."

They exchanged uneasy glances as they puffed their cigarettes.

The sky was smoky and sinister as their stale tobacco rose.

The Human Fish felt more betrayed and undervalued than ever.

A caged animal trapped in his own courtesy.

He wanted to howl like a dog.

He wanted to express his inner conflict, to make Jim feel how he felt, unhinged.

He was like an infant, tripping over his own feet into the next moment improving with every fall and smiling hysterically.

A baby with its maker.

He remembered what Destiny said.

"People are born as tiny wrinkled fetuses and leave possessed by demons."

He had to have faith that Jim wouldn't get him arrested or worse.

It was do-or-die.

They'd pursue this brief and savage wilderness together, and hopefully, he'd live to tell the tale.

Otherwise, he'd be just another dead fish, deceived into thinking he was more by the trickery of man.

8

The Human Fish's organs stretched as he extended into the box.

His bones cracked as he rolled around, trying to get comfortable.

It was far from cozy, unspecified objects sticking between his crevices.

Hopefully no guns, he thought.

Boredom made him think strange thoughts.

He imagined swimming in deep coves and playing Frisbee with starfish.

He imagined pearls of whale ejaculate floating to the surface.

It made him miss the permeable and indeterminate space of the road.

His body went crazy for something to do.

He was physically hungry but felt a deeper hunger beneath it all.

His soul was shrieking to escape.

His psyche was turning to drywall and cracking.

The only way to regain some sense of freedom was through a car wreck.

The load would flip endlessly over itself, and he would be free in a crapshoot of death.

Rain hit the tin roof, and the Human Fish imagined he was back in the ocean, in a turtle's shell, nestled and safe.

Finally, they stopped, and the Human Fish waited for the signal.

Three knocks from Jim to indicate they were clear.

The door opened, and he heard footsteps, breaking the spell.

Jim cracked the box open with a crowbar and lifted the top off.

"I think it was the rain that saved us. None of those shlubs wanted to search the trailer in the rain."

By the time they got out of the truck, it was well past midnight.

They stopped at a bed and breakfast to rest.

It was a small log cabin at the top of a hill and looked more inviting than the motels.

The front of the cabin had large triangular windows overlooking the forest and beyond, like an observatory.

There was a line of cars parked on the front lawn, and a gravel driveway that Jim pulled into.

The truck's headlights reflected off the glass and made the whole house glow.

The Human Fish saw the owner shuffle to the front door and prop it open.

He was an old man wearing a bathrobe and smoking a pipe.

He had receding cheekbones and a tuft of white hair on the dimple of his chin.

He was wearing sunglasses despite it being black as pitch.

His wrinkled brow scrunched his face when he smiled.

"Come in, my friends. Come in," he said, with a friendly smile.

They hurried inside and followed the owner to the front desk.

Jim asked, "This your place, grandpa? Got any rooms available?"

The owner shuffled through some papers at the desk and shook his head.

"There are no rooms available, but there is a backyard. A few acres worth where you can make camp. There are hammocks where you can sleep, an outhouse where you can shit, and a freestanding shower where you can cleanse yourself of your journey."

The owner removed his sunglasses.

He slid them in front of a fluorescent ceiling light.

It cast an eerie, segmented shadow across the room.

The owner fidgeted with the frames, which made for a bouncing illusion that was hypnotic.

The Human Fish could see the whites of his eyes.

He was blind.

He spoke with an unusual cadence that the Human Fish found hard to parse.

His voice seemed to come in and out like a crackling radio signal.

Occasional phrases cut through.

And then it was as if the storm had cleared and his words became clear.

"You have traveled a long and arduous road to be here," he said. "Off the beaten path, and through the wilderness, you have gone. You seek answers, and you will get them, though they will not be the answers you were looking for. You will see everything there is to see, in this godforsaken country. One day you will rule it all, like a king without a crown. This will be a pilgrimage of paradoxes, a journey of the ins and outs, pleasure and pain. Though you may wish to race to the end of the road like the hare, you must keep the pace of the turtle. Slowly find your way, for the obstacles that will come must be taken with great care. Or else, you will find yourself a ghost."

The Human Fish was stunned.

He could feel the whites of the man's eyes wrapped around him like fog.

He didn't move or say anything.

Jim stood off to the side, confused.

Cranberry was snoring on a couch by the entrance.

The owner of the bed and breakfast smiled.

"Enough chitchat," he said. "You need to rest. Let me show you where you'll sleep."

There were lanterns and mosquito torches lighting the way.

Beyond the porch were hammocks, and a fire pit that was smoking from recent use.

The blind owner knew his way and showed them to their lodging.

"I leave you here," he said. "I hope you enjoy your time here. It will be the last comfortable sleep you have for a long time. Trouble is brewing. Your best bet is to turn around and go back to where you came from. I know you won't, but I have to say it. Get some sleep. Goodnight."

Jim laughed after the owner was out of sight.

"Can you believe that old coot?" he asked. "What the hell was he talking about in there? He's more fucked up than I am."

The Human Fish was only half listening.

He was thinking about the journey, how the worst was yet to come.

Cranberry chased fireflies around, huffing and puffing through the grass.

The Human Fish hung in the hammock and felt like a spider in the middle of a world-sized cobweb.

The moon hung in a sparkling white curve, the sprawling muddy plain lit in shadowy stains.

The only noise was the chirping of the crickets and throaty groans of toads.

The sky was punctuated by constellations.

He savored the moment of openness with nothing dividing him from his surroundings.

He felt the naked energy of the universe buzzing all around.

He could feel the ocean's tide calling to him, heard the words, "Go back to the sea."

As much as he might want to, the trip was not yet over.

The next morning the Human Fish was greeted with a punch of wind to the face.

The temperature plummeted, and he was shivering.

The sky was gray.

It was a misty day.

His scales were making a chattering sound.

He looked around for Jim and found him back in the truck.

The Human Fish needed to hydrate and wanted to take a shower.

He settled for dumping a half liter of Coca-Cola on his chest.

The sugar made his torso gluey and stick to the seatbelt.

"What are you doing," asked Jim. "You need to get back into the trailer, remember?"

The Human fish undid the seatbelt and opened the door.

Jim stuck the keys in the ignition, and the engine idled.

"After this checkpoint, we're home free."

The animal part of his brain, the instinctual part that had no sense of reasoning, told the Human Fish to go home.

The human part of his brain was telling him the same, but his heart told him to go on.

If the owner of the bed and breakfast was right, he could not stop until his journey was complete.

The Human Fish climbed inside the crate and curled up in the fetal position like an embryo in utero.

He felt more like he was inside of a whale's anus, queasy and suffocating.

The plastic sheeting wormed its way into his flesh.

He would only have to breathe in the stench of exhaust for a little while longer.

He clenched his muscles as tight as they could go, ignoring the cramps.

The tension pulsed through his limbs and he ground his sharp sets of teeth like scissors.

He opened his eyes and let his body slacken, taking the deepest breath he could.

The best option he had was to sleep.

He closed his eyes and kicked his arms and legs violently.

He tried to get comfortable but was barely able to move an inch.

Eventually, after a few hours in traffic, he dozed off.

9

The truck screeched to a halt, and the boxes rolled around the back of the trailer like tumbling dice.

The Human Fish woke mid-air.

He tried not to throw up from the bile splashing against his stomach like waves against the hull of a ship.

He tuned his otoliths and listened to the movements outside.

He heard the mutterings of Jim.

There was a deeper voice, with hints of scorn and cynicism, ordering him to stay put.

There was a crunch-crunch-crunch of heavy feet, a squeal of metal as the trailer opened.

He imagined the beasts approaching, body-armored hairy ogres thirsty for blood.

Then he heard the sound of barking as the drug-sniffing dog caught the scent of the first box.

He heard the sound of a crowbar prying apart the wood block.

He started to sweat.

He heard the light tapping of the dog's feet getting closer.

Its bark hurt his ears.

Fuck, he thought.

Dogs were like demons.

They could smell fear.

He could feel the drug-sniffing dog pawing the box, rocking it back and forth and barking.

The more the dog barked, the more the Human Fish sweat and the more the dog tried to tear through to ravage him.

It took a group of officers to pull the dog away, and they used a crowbar to pry the box open.

They reached in and upon seeing the Human Fish, started to bark unintelligibly like the dog.

They lifted him up and slammed him face-first into the floor.

The Human Fish had been a victim of the police before, but it never involved such physical pain.

He remembered how it felt to be locked in that cold cell.

That now seemed like paradise compared to being shoved in a box in the back of a moving truck.

He knew that the only way he'd get out alive would be to play the role of the victim.

So that's what he did.

He turned traitor in an instant.

He screamed, "Help me, I've been fishnapped!"

Within seconds, the Human Fish built a story about how Jim stole him from his mother and was keeping him hostage.

Then instinct told him what to do; he groveled on the ground and blubbered that he wanted his mother.

The police drug him out on his belly.

They emptied the pockets of his swim trunks.

They removed his goggles, his flippers, checking every orifice for contraband.

The Human Fish cried salty tears made from the ocean itself.

The police put him in a separate car as Jim, and a few seconds later Cranberry joined him in the back seat.

He took this as a good sign, and pet the dog.

Cranberry snapped, bearing his teeth and growling.

It was more aggression that the Human Fish had ever seen out of the dog.

The police separated them once they reached the jail.

They put him in a small room with a table in the middle and chairs on either side.

The Human Fish couldn't sit down.

He was too nervous.

Eventually, a man in a suit joined him in the room.

He introduced himself as Special Agent.

But before Special Agent could ask a single question, the Human Fish asked for a lawyer.

He knew how the game was played from his first time in jail.

He wasn't about to spend a night in a cell with a deranged clown.

The lawyer didn't look very reassuring.

His shirt was untucked, and he was sweating worse than the Human Fish.

But when they got down to talking, the lawyer was

a force to be reckoned.

He told the police that the Human Fish was caught up in a conspiracy beyond his ignorant comprehension.

He used some other derogatory language, but the Human Fish didn't care.

He was impressed by how the lawyer spoke on his behalf, so persuasively.

It made him want to defend people, to have the power to save someone from their demise.

The lawyer said that the Human Fish was trapped without water or food.

He was being transported with illegal imports as if he was contraband.

Clearly, he said, Jim thought that a half-man, half-fish would fetch a good price at market.

The Human Fish stared at the ceiling having no idea where he was going after this, or if he could leave.

It made him realize how much he needed to see his mother.

If he had to spend the rest of his life in a box, he would be devastated at the lack of closure.

In the morning, the sun split and stretching the bars like an octopus being birthed.

He was greeted by a guard.

Once again, it was his lucky day.

He was released, a victim, dehydrated and hungry.

This time, there weren't protestors waiting outside of the jail.

It was an empty slab surrounded by a chain-link fence with barbed wire and bird's nests up above.

The Human Fish walked down the concrete runway toward the parking lot.

Beyond was a wooded area with picnic tables and a banner that said, "Welcome home, Fred!"

Balloons, streamers, and other decorations embellished the area with bright colors.

A group of hunchbacked people was meandering around.

Some of them appeared to be digging.

They had long black hair that hung over their faces and talon-like nails encrusted in dirt.

They were pulling up thick earthworms as dense as forearms, and putting them on plates to eat.

They were mole people.

They couldn't see the Human Fish, but they could smell his sadness and desperation.

They asked if he wanted to join their feast.

He sat down, and they introduced themselves.

Fred was paroled after serving the maximum sentence for armed robbery.

He would have been let out early, but his sentence was extended on account that he kept trying to burrow out.

They chopped up an earthworm and offered the Human Fish the end piece, as he was the guest.

It was still squirming.

Fred was sitting at the head of the table, with the head of the worm.

It was a mouthwatering meal compared to the indigestible gruel he'd been eating.

When Fred finished devouring the grubs on his plate, he asked the Human Fish about himself.

It may have been the meal, but the Human Fish felt entirely comfortable divulging his entire tale.

If anything, he thought, Fred deserved a good story on his birthday.

He detailed every nuance of his journey.

At one point he broke down into tears, and the mole people patted their paws on his shoulders and nuzzled him.

Some of the others, seeing Fred all alone at the end of the table, being upstaged on his big day, went over to nuzzle him too.

But Fred seemed just fine with the situation.

He didn't say much, but when he did speak, his words burrowed into the Human Fish like a drill.

"You need closure," Fred said. "You had a relationship that didn't pan out the way you wanted it to, and he left before you could say goodbye. I think you need to say goodbye."

The Human Fish thought about his mother, and Destiny, and all of the people who he had left without a proper goodbye.

He came so far just to fill a void left by Jim, and if he didn't fill it now, he never would.

Facing him would be scary, but he'd come this far.

He'd worn clothing, faced danger, and neutered his own existence just so that the humans would accept him.

He was done trying to be accepted by humans.

The mole people were another story.

Their hospitality was unprecedented.

They offered the Human Fish a piece of worm to take with him.

His appetite was gone, but he took the piece anyway.

He chucked it against the windshield of a parked police car.

Guts splattered back on his face, and he remembered what the little boy who asked him for an autograph said.

How he called him scary when he saw the ketchup on his face.

So he licked the guts off his cheeks.

He wiped his face off and walked back around the prison.

He asked to see Jim.

10

Jim looked even worse than usual.

Stubble grew in the crevice of his double-chins like pubic hair between ass cheeks.

He looked like a castaway.

There was crust in his eyes, and he was drooling but didn't wipe it off.

The Human Fish picked up the plastic phone.

Jim had a devious smile and empty eyes.

"I want to tell you a story," he said. "I used to have hemorrhoids. Being on the road, my eating habits weren't the best. One day I noticed the blood in my stool, and the little peanut-sized veins poking out my rear. They grew to the size of overripe strawberries. I had a long delivery to make, and I didn't know how I was gonna do it. I couldn't even sit down, the pain was so bad. So you know what I did? I mixed a bunch of oxys with some wild turkey. I took a razor blade and a tiny hand mirror, and I cut those hemorrhoids off myself. I left those bloody anal beads on the floor of the motel bathroom, and drove cross-country the next day without looking back."

Jim leaned in closer to the window.

"To me, Igor, you're no different than those goddamn hemorrhoids."

The Human Fish was taken aback.

He didn't expect such an assault upon visiting the man who locked him in a wooden crate.

At first, he felt confusion, then anger.

It was always there, in the shallows of his psyche, but now it was ripping its way to the surface.

He felt a fury within him like the crashing of a thousand waves.

He took off his goggles and felt the oxygen's pressure.

He opened his eyes wide and felt his corneas pulsing.

They bled down his face like a pair of open scabs.

The Human Fish leaned toward Jim.

He wiped the blood from his face onto the glass.

Then the waves came crashing down, and the Human Fish spoke more than he ever had before.

"You abandoned me, and I did everything for you. I hate you. You're worse than anything out of the deepest depths of the ocean. I should have stayed with mom. You fucker. You abandoned us both. You ruined everything. I could have been normal. Normal enough, at least. I never would have been human, and I never would have been a fish. But at least I would have had support. I would have been my best self. But how could I with you as my father? You're a liar and a thief. You're the scum of the earth. I hope you rot in prison. Eat shit and die."

His hair was sticking up on end, and his veins were wriggling like electric eels.

He wanted to ram his skull through the glass and strangle Jim.

There are some lives you live, and some you leave behind.

The Human Fish was ready to close this path on his journey.

Jim didn't seem so ready.

He was blinking erratically.

He opened his mouth and closed it repeatedly.

His hot breath fogged up the glass.

He grabbed his chest, heart under siege, tipping back in his chair and clattering to the floor.

The Human Fish called for help from the guard.

The guard was tall and muscular and pale, with a face like hairy mutton pumped full of growth hormone.

In meat spirit, he was more like pork though, with the dry taste of turkey.

He liked to make deadpan jokes at the inmates' expense, and never so much as cracked a smile.

He looked down at Jim and said, "I guess you didn't know. This isn't a hospital."

Despite his anger, the Human Fish was mortified by the guard's lack of sympathy.

He tried to ask another guard, but he was equally uncaring.

A few in-prison nurses came and lugged Jim away.

They guaranteed he would be fine but exchanged concerned glances.

As the Human Fish was escorted out, he heard a familiar sound.

It was the neigh of an iron horse.

He saw a woman clad in leather pull into the parking lot.

Removing her helmet, she was the most beautiful woman he had ever seen.

It was Destiny.

She ran toward the Human Fish like she was going to tackle him.

At the last second, she let her arms go and embraced him.

It sounded like she was crying, and it wasn't until she leaned back that the Human Fish saw her face.

She was laughing.

The Human Fish told her everything that happened, but she already knew.

She knew everything about Cristiano.

She said that Jim used her to get to him so that he could move drugs.

It was his master plan to use his stripper daughter to get to the kingpin.

She asked where Jim was.

He said that he was inside.

He said that the guards could still bring him back if she wanted to speak with him.

Destiny told him that his incarceration was closure enough.

She said that she was really there to pick up Cranberry.

The Human Fish wondered how she would transport a dog on her motorcycle.

Destiny answered for him.

"You can carry Cranberry on the way home."

The Human Fish didn't know how he would

manage to carry a dog and remain on the motorcycle.

Then he remembered the leash.

They walked back around the prison to pick up Cranberry.

They passed the field where the mole people had their barbeque.

There were a group of prison guards posted up around the perimeter.

They were yelling back and forth with the family.

They ordered the mole people to take the festivities elsewhere.

The mole people held their ground.

They declared that the park was public and they could do whatever they wanted there.

Battle lines were drawn.

Tension grew.

The prison guards drew their batons.

The mole people clutched their plastic eating utensils.

Pandemonium ensued, skulls cracking and eyeballs scooped out.

Fred charged with multiple forks in each hand and caught a guard in the ribs like he was shanking an inmate.

The melee went on until both sides were bloody piles of beaten bodies.

Destiny took the Human Fish away when the snipers started firing upon the mole people.

They were mowing them down.

The Human Fish held his hands up and wrapped himself over Destiny like a shield.

He didn't want any stray bullets to kill his sister.

She was an angel that the world couldn't afford to lose.

Several of the mole people were chasing after them. They were yelling for help, but it was too late.

Their fate was sealed as soon as the snipers reloaded.

The Human Fish and Destiny made it to the other side, picked up Cranberry, and drove off into the sunset.

He held the old gray dog as they glided down the highway.

The dog was leashed to his neck, so if he dropped him, they would both die.

They drove for miles and miles, days and days.

They drove past farmlands with cows grazing and horses running free.

Past paraplegic hitchhikers in wheelchairs barely able to hold their thumbs out for a ride.

The Human Fish heard the words, "Go back to the sea," and he planned to.

As soon he got off this wild ride.

11

Destiny dropped the Human Fish off at his apartment.

Destiny tied the leash around Cranberry's neck and drove away.

After Destiny left, the Human Fish couldn't shake the feeling that he was being followed.

He felt like he could be blindsided at any moment by some ferocious and bloodthirsty beast.

There was an ominous cloud in his periphery.

His blood raced as he prayed for rain, something to cool his spirit down.

A car pulled down the alley behind him, and he started to shake.

His whole nervous system ticked like a bomb counting down to detonation.

His instincts screeched a warning that his brain couldn't comprehend.

The car doors opened, and a pair of shadowy figures exited the back.

The Human Fish didn't look.

He walked fast, fumbling his keys as he neared the entrance to his apartment.

He dropped them next to the dumpster, and just as he went to pick them up, they appeared before him.

The first man adjusted the strap so that his eyes fit with the holes of the ski mask.

The second man took a pistol out of his waistband.

He checked the chamber before cocking it.

He aimed the barrel at the Human Fish's face.

Then the first man grabbed him from behind.

The Human Fish tried to kick and flail to get away, but the muscle-bound assailants were too powerful.

He could smell their testosterone and pumped up masculinity.

They were bred for this.

They blindfolded him and threw him in the trunk of their car.

They drove for a while and eventually pulled him back out.

He couldn't see anything, but he could smell.

It reeked of blood and flesh and congealed tissue.

There was a familiar scent underneath it, that of a woman.

An unknown pair of hands untied the blindfold.

The Human Fish found himself in the middle of an abandoned slaughterhouse.

Two Hell's Angels were standing over a meat grinder in the middle of the room.

Its rotary blades were spinning.

They were holding Destiny upside down by her ankles over the blade.

Sitting in front of the meat grinder was a man with oil-slicked hair and brown moles all over his face.

"We should have brought a broiler for the fish," he said, and the Hell's Angels laughed.

"We can make do with what we have."

On the floor, there were pliers, a blowtorch, and a chainsaw.

"Have a seat," said the oily man, gesturing to a chair across from him.

The Human Fish sat down.

"I know who you are," he said. "My name is Cristiano. I'm sure you've heard about me."

The Human Fish had indeed heard of Cristiano and could see the blood in his eyes like a shark on the hunt.

They were equal stature, but for some reason Cristiano seemed a few heads taller than him.

He asked the Human Fish about the drugs and Jim Hurley.

The Human Fish told him that they were arrested and the drugs were taken.

Cristiano said, "True, but why is Jim still in prison, and you're free?"

The Human Fish said "I don't know," and Cristiano shook his head.

He talked about what would happen next.

"You're in trouble. Very serious trouble. Dead in the water."

Cristiano reached down and picked up the blowtorch.

He turned on the gas and pulled the trigger.

"How does it make you feel," asked Cristiano.

"Afraid," the Human Fish said.

It seemed like Cristiano wanted him to feel afraid, but actually he felt fine.

Fire didn't scare fish the way it scared humans.

"I bet it does. You're a bitch. You snitched, and it's time to pay the price. Would you agree with this assessment?"

"Probably," the Human Fish said.

Then after a few seconds, he smiled and said, "Not."

Cristiano stood up and said, "You're dead, fish. So fucking dead."

The Human Fish wondered what it would feel like if Cristiano slipped and accidentally burned him in the face.

What if it felt like someone taking his picture, really awkward and feeling compelled to smile as the flame left the chamber and burned its way through his skull.

"I didn't snitch, honestly," the Human Fish said, "but if you're going to kill me, then just get it over with."

Cristiano laughed.

"Oh no, I'm gonna take my time with," but the Human Fish didn't wait for him to finish.

He knocked the blowtorch out of Cristiano's hand.

He tackled him to the floor, and said, "Nobody move or I'll kill him."

The Hell's Angel's dropped Destiny and ran toward the Human Fish.

The bigger of the aggressors took a wild swing and missed.

The Human Fish dodged the punch, ducked, and dove in a desperate effort to grab one of the weapons.

He looked at the array of tools and grabbed the pliers.

The Human Fish cinched the pliers around the bigger biker's nose and broke it in the clamp.

Not just broke it, obliterated it.

He clenched his eyes and squeezed until there was nothing left but an empty sinus cavity.

The next biker attacked, but the Human Fish was ready.

He somersaulted forward, dove, and bit the biker in his calf.

He clamped down with his my might, just like he'd learned from the mother rat.

The biker let out a wild squeal and tried to pull himself from the Human Fish's clutches, but it was too late.

He dug deeper with his teeth.

He pulverized the flesh between his molars.

The inner animal was off its reins.

He was a predator on the fringe of insanity.

He was half-smiling.

He was ready to dismember with his bare hands.

There was no real technique involved, but he was winning.

He grabbed the biker's balls.

The biker fell to his knees, and the Human Fish looked into his eyes.

It was as if his soul had left his body.

His cry sounded distant.

The Human Fish twisted the sack, and it was as if the soul was coaxed back.

With his free hand, he reached down and grabbed the blowtorch.

Gas hissed from the nozzle, and then there was fire.

Just then the noseless biker went to swing at him.

The Human Fish grabbed, twisted, wrestled, the other biker as a human shield.

He unhinged his jaw, brought the blowtorch up and melted the biker's face like candlewax.

Destiny jumped on the other biker's back and choked him.

She reached her arm under his chin and locked her hand behind his head.

It was like a rodeo, being thrashed around while she held on, trying not to be thrown to her doom.

Eventually, the biker's legs buckled.

He let out one final grunt before collapsing.

But that still wasn't the end.

Cristiano gave the Human Fish a punch to the face, followed by a devastating elbow to spine.

The pain nearly knocked him unconscious.

He dropped to his knees and prepared for the final blow, but that's when he saw the chainsaw.

The Human Fish swung the chainsaw in self-defense, chewing through Cristiano's jugular with the teeth of the blade.

Nerve bundles vibrated and popped.

The flesh ruptured, and blood bubbles burst from the split.

The Human Fish caught Cristiano as he fell.

He reached into his neck and pinched shut the severed artery.

Dark red sinewy flesh wriggled around his wrist.

He tightened his grip as the throat splintered from the shoulders like a tree trunk with severed roots.

He needed answers.

Cristiano didn't stay conscious long enough.

The blood supply to his brain was disconnected, and he slowly faded until he was gone.

The human didn't move, and neither did Destiny.

They were both in shock.

Eventually, they recovered enough to silently dispose of the evidence.

They threw the bodies in the meat grinder and let it chew them up.

Blood was everywhere.

Feet of intestines were chopped and oozing feces.

Eviscerated organs lay still pulsing over piles of bone fragment.

They scooped it all up with their bare hands, into transparent plastic wrap they found in the trunk of the car.

They secured the giant ball of guts with duct tape and closed the trunk back up.

"Are you going to be okay," asked Destiny, her voice cracking with trauma.

"I'm fine," he said.

The Human Fish ached, but beyond a baseball-sized lump on his head, a dislocated jaw, and several impacted teeth, he would live.

Destiny was unscathed aside from the bruises around her ankles from being hung upside down.

She made a fool of death with her beauty.

They parted ways without another word, Destiny in Cristiano's car, the Human Fish in the bikers'.

He drove to a sea that was calling him home, but for a different purpose.

To drop dead men's guts into the abyss.

It was easier than he thought.

He blinked, and the sharks were there.

The frenzy that ensued was a tornado of teeth and gore.

The tide carried out a steady current of blood and bone.

The Human Fish stared out at the ocean.

The womb that birthed him.

It was something powerful to behold.

The whole planet depended on its existence, each ebb and flow causing wind and rain and natural disaster.

The Human Fish hoped that, with its might and sovereignty, that it might absolve him.

But despite the sea's strength, he knew that it could not forgive the violence of man.

It was destined to succumb and be violated by the hands from above.

He stood barefoot in the shell-encrusted sand, beyond which was endless water.

There were trawlers in the distance; nets thick with fish heaved high by winches on the verge of snapping.

A crab emerged for mere seconds before the tide washed it away.

The ghostly silhouettes of the sharks glided away and vanished into the darkness of the reef.

The Human Fish looked down and saw his ankles covered in a sheet of frothing water.

He trudged forward until he was up to his waist.

He looked back at the gray expanse of the city and forward at the blue water.

He removed his goggles, took a deep breath, and went under.

12

Destiny took the Human Fish out for coffee.

It'd been years since they'd seen each other, out of fear that Cristiano's thugs might still be watching out for them.

The Human Fish looked different.

His hair was freshly cut and quaffed.

He was dressed in a suit.

There was a hole in the back of his suit with a dorsal fin poking through.

It had grown in some sort of late-stage puberty and made wearing a shirt even more uncomfortable.

Destiny looked different too.

Her skin was bright and unmarked.

She'd sold Jim's truck and used the money to get her tattoos removed.

She said that she wanted to start over.

Her flesh was taught and pink.

She was recently accepted into the Peace Corps and was moving to Morocco later that month.

The Human Fish was living in the nation's capital, where he attended law school.

He loved being a lawyer.

Court trials were like being in a controlled firefight.

It was a fierce battle in which lives were at stake.

One team was meant to give life, and the other was expected to take it away.

The Human Fish approached the legal system with instinct and assertiveness and panache.

He wasn't respected by the authorities the way that the other lawyers were.

It wasn't that they went out of their way to offend him, but more that they disregarded his existence.

As a result, he glided under the radar like a stingray beneath the sand.

He struck when they least expected it.

He'd gained an outsider's perspective to the world of man and knew of their innate failures.

He knew all about the corruption of the legal system, the sleaziness of politics and backroom bribery.

And he was determined to put an end to all of it, to fix humanity in his own way, in his own time.

Outside of the coffee shop, a man was handing out slips of paper that said, "Show this card at any participating area Exxon station to get your free 'Save the Blue Whale' bumper sticker."

The man was wearing Jesus sandals, and his feet were well manicured.

Every so often the sun caught his toenails at just the right angle, refracting prisms of light along the cuticles.

There was something about this man, those clenched hands, the set of his jaw, that made him look incredibly tense.

Suddenly the weather became overcast, and the man's toenails stopped glowing.

Drizzle landed next to his feet, and the sky opened up in an explosive downpour.

Even as the storm barraged him, the man just stood there with his hand out, holding a soggy card that collapsed under the weight of a thousand raindrops.

A flash of lightning struck the horizon, thunder within the same second, and the Human Fish worried about the safety of this man.

He was part of an endangered species that the planet could not afford to lose.

Destiny grabbed a piece of paper from the man's hand.

"I need gas anyway," she said.

Destiny drove the Human Fish back to her place.

She stopped off to refuel and pasted the blue whale bumper sticker on the side of her hog.

When they got back to the house, it was completely different than the Human Fish remembered, as was the old gray dog, now a young, black pup.

His patchy fur grew back, and his breath stopped smelling so bad.

Destiny poured Cranberry his dinner and scattered chunks of beef on top of his kibble.

He was regenerating, becoming stronger.

All of them were being resurrected.

Brought back from the brink of destruction.

With Jim out of the picture, they were all living their best lives.

It was as if the antidote for the poison of their lives was discovered.

The weeds were pulled.

There was a garden out front flourishing.

The house no longer smelled like rotting flesh.

It smelled of incense.

The entire place had a disinfected shine.

Destiny kept a journal of her days, each subtle improvement tallied.

Every trouble surmounted was accounted for.

She explained her choice to become a vegan.

She believed that animals were purer than humans.

Yet, since last seeing one another, both Destiny and the Human Fish had been domesticated.

He didn't reject the change.

He did sometimes miss the swell of ocean life, how alive he felt in the vast and endless space.

Though his memory was fragmented and blurred.

He was having a hard time remembering what came first, the world of fish or the world of man.

That was the reason he came back to Los Angeles, for closure.

"Come on," he told Destiny, "I want to show you something."

He gave her directions, and she drove to the shore.

Destiny sat with her legs crossed at the edge of the surf, staring out at the horizon.

The color of the sky was a warm violet.

The ocean was a deep red.

It looks like a glass of blood.

It was the color that the ocean turned when there was electricity in the air, and a storm was coming.

There were bursts of wiry gold lightning here and there, but no sound of thunder that could surpass the sound of the waves.

The Human Fish took it all in.

His half-fish form embraced the intricacies of the human body, but it never stopped being part of the ocean.

He imagined melting into the foam, the border between body and sea gone.

The one place he had yet to explore was the sky.

He vowed to one day fly, to see everything from above.

To become a spirit of the air.

A flock of seagulls soared.

They were like grains of sand caught in the mighty current of life.

It was an undulating landscape collapsing into itself over and over again for eternity.

As if this was routine destruction.

Misshaping and reforming.

The planet roared through space and time, yet there they were, in the heart of it all.

Among countless other bodies in the titanic whirlpool of the galaxy.

"Our father was a piece of shit," Destiny said, "Like his manipulation. He used to lock me in the basement as a child, and every time I went upstairs, he acted like it was a treat to be in the world. I would obsess over it. I'd come out of the darkness and never knew what was real or fake."

She squinted as if trying very hard to focus on some distant memory.

"Once he took me to the ocean. It was my birthday, and he took me to the ocean as my gift. And there were hundreds of dead jellyfish washed up on the shore.

I couldn't stop thinking about it. Every time I was locked back in the darkness, I saw them, electric hearts throbbing through their translucent skin."

The Human Fish didn't know what to say.

He stood in the shallow coastal water with a whole country of land between himself and the next ocean.

There was an airplane passing overhead with a banner that read, "Jean, will you marry me?"

Red petals of fire hung behind it, a flower of burning gas that was expanding as it sunk.

The Human Fish wondered what his ancestors would think of the present.

The sea was humbled by man's selfish presumption that it was theirs.

Yet they failed to preserve anything.

The reef was dying.

In return, each year, the sea claimed victims that fell into its jaws.

The waves roared, and the Human Fish glimpsed the head of a trout poke briefly up from the surf, winking at him.

He put his arm around Destiny's shoulder and pointed.

"That's my mom," he said smiling.

Destiny smiled, held his hand, and waved.

The Human Fish's worlds were colliding, and slowly, he was coming to terms with the result.

When at last they rose, the sun had already fallen down the other side of the sky.

A full moon was in its place, shedding beacons of light upon the shore.

It felt like a crucial moment for both of them.

The type of moment that might be considered fate.

The wind picked up, and rain began to fall.

A thunderclap shook the shore.

People were fleeing for safety under the dock.

Beach umbrellas flew above the dunes.

Destiny held him close.

She was gazing up into the western sky, examining the outer layer of her universe.

One by one, the stars sprang to life.

The storm passed and the clouds cleared.

The light amassed and blended with the darkness in a collage over the beach.

The only people left there were Destiny and the Human Fish.

He was staring at the constellation of Pisces, the plural of fish, and in his opinion, the most beautiful alignment of stars.

It was drifting toward Aquarius, the water-carrier.

A trillion-mile-high orbit governed by gravity.

The earth spun dizzily in space.

As the minutes passed, it seemed to twirl faster and faster on its axis, threatening to launch him like a rock launched from a slingshot.

He buried his feet in the sand and clung with his toes.

But the surface was grainy and gave him no refuge.

He could die at any sudden twist.

But he held on anyway, because life was worth holding on for.

13

One night, the Human Fish had a dream.

In the dream, there was a whale, in the deepest, darkest depths of the ocean.

It seemed like an ordinary whale from the outside, but there was more at work than met the eye.

Inside of the whale was a man, in a steel chamber confined within the whale's skull.

Their brains were connected through the cerebellum by wires of stringy flesh.

The man was using the whale to protect him from harm but was also controlling it.

When he turned his head left, the whale went left.

When he turned his head right, the whale went right.

Outside of the whale were all kinds of explosives and booby-trapped harpoons.

The whale was impaled and exploded but continued to chug ahead.

It kept going until it slid onto the shore and the

man exited out of its mouth.

The whale was in pieces that the man harvested and used to feed his family.

Then, when they were hungry again, the man returned to the ocean.

Another whale swallowed him, and the process repeated.

The Human Fish woke with an epiphany.

It was like reaching an end that was also a beginning.

Like a rapid expansion of matter exploding from a state of nothingness.

Stabilizing at a time-bending speed.

The dream spurred the Human Fish's imagination to generate a utopia where man and fish coexisted.

No longer would the water, nor the dry land be shunned.

The planet would be one central place of origin.

With his newfound plan, the Human Fish got into politics.

The Human Fish became the president of four different nations at the same time.

He started as the mayor of California and gained attention by creating a trash economy.

The abundance of the world's trash was a growing concern, and he had the solution.

To use cubes of trash as money.

Everyone became rich.

It was like a second gold rush.

The Human Fish used the money for good.

He bought food for the hungry.

He bought shelter for the homeless.

He bought clothes for the naked.

He bought parents for the orphans.

He bought peace on earth.

He bought liberty and justice for all.

There was no more war, no more soldiers being blown apart in trenches or chemical warfare or nuclear holocausts.

Those evils vanished from the public mind.

That single idea stabilized the nation, and it wasn't long before the Human Fish was president over four different countries, and his plans were being put into play.

The population multiplied as a new race emerged, half-human, half-fish creatures that possessed the best traits of either species.

They breathed water like fish, grew scales on their flesh, webbing between their toes, and fins on their backs.

They were still carnivores.

Until there was a half-man, half-chicken to lobby for the meat community, meat was fair game.

The ocean, much of it had yet to be explored by man until then.

They built underwater cities, more magnificent than Atlantis.

The land became more plentiful with life than ever.

Underwater wasn't that different from above.

They both had patterns of dirt and sand that repeated over and over, with infinite variations.

Yet, each day presented a new challenge to the Human Fish.

He explored both worlds, treading through the concrete forests and the sea.

The most significant similarity he saw was when he was in a clearing.

Beyond the tangle of trees, the grass swaying in the wind was much like the ocean's waves pulsing.

It was then that he had the idea to end world hunger.

He ended the famine that scourged all living creatures for ages, but which would never threaten the world again as long as there were sea farms harvesting sea salads filled with protein and other nutrients.

Until the tide ceased, they would never be hungry again.

Everything used solar power.

The sun was God.

The Human Fish sought to use his abilities from both worlds to bridge space and cleanse the universe of evil.

He planned to build a space colony on a planet with water, maybe Mars, where everyone could start over with fresh resources.

The world would be a fish bowl.

He would create utopias across the galaxy.

Across the universe.

He was a strong, resilient individual toughened by years of peril.

He'd survived altercations unimaginable to most.

He was universally admired.

People came from all around the world to sit at his feet and gain wisdom from his knowledge.

He'd been through the circles of hell and emerged enlightened.

He was the messiah of religious texts.

And the Human Fish could feel the lives of billions around him.

Water consumed the world like one giant sea spilling across all surfaces.

Every creature grew stronger from the water.

Water was everything.

Humans were oceans.

Earth was a giant orb of crystal blue glowing from the center.

But that glow wasn't there until the Human Fish was born.

Before that, there was only darkness.

Now, there was light.

ABOUT THE AUTHOR

Benjamin DeVos is the author of The Bar Is Low, Lord of the Game, and Madness Has a Moment and Then Vanishes Before Returning Again. He is the head editor of Apocalypse Party and lives in Philadelphia.